D0065836

Under the Big Sky

WRITTEN AND ILLUSTRATED BY

TREVOR ROMAIN

SCHOLASTIC INC.
New York Toronto London Auckland Sydney
Mexico City New Delhi Hong Kong Buenos Aires

ISBN 0-439-41168-8

Text copyright © 1993 by Trevor Romain.
Illustrations copyright © 2001 by Trevor Romain.
All rights reserved.
Published by Scholastic Inc., 557 Broadway, New York, NY 10012,
by arrangement with HarperCollins Publishers.
SCHOLASTIC and associated logos are trademarks and/or
registered trademarks of Scholastic Inc.

12 11 10 9 8 7 6 5 4 3 2 1   2 3 4 5 6 7/0

Printed in Mexico   49

First Scholastic printing, April 2002

Typography by Stephanie Bart-Horvath

To my dad, who gave me everything
under the big sky.
—T.R.

One afternoon, an old man said to his grandson, "I am getting old and one of these days I'm going to die. I would like you to have all my riches once I am gone. But before you have them, you must find the secret of life and bring it back to me."

"But Grandfather, where will I find the secret
of life?" asked the young boy.

"Under the big sky," said the grandfather.
"You'll find it under the big sky."

So with his mind filled with dreams of future wealth, the young boy set out to find the secret of life. Before long he came upon a car.

"Excuse me," he said to the car. "Did you perhaps pass the secret of life on your way over here?"

"Nope," said the car. "Never ran across the secret of life myself, but I will tell you one thing. No matter how many miles you travel, you should always remember where you came from."

The young boy thanked the car and traveled
farther until he came upon a tree.

He spoke to the top of the tree. "Can you see the secret of life from up there?"

"I can only see the tops of other oaks," said the tree. "But I do have some advice for you."

"Please tell me," said the boy. "I need some good advice."

The tree said, "Always make certain your roots are firmly planted in the ground, because the winds of change will try to knock you down."

The boy took the advice and moved on.

He searched high. . . .

He searched low. . . .

He even searched in the library.
But he did not find the secret of life.

The boy continued his journey and
met a farmer in a field.

"You look lost," said the farmer.

"I'm looking for the secret of life," said the boy, glancing around.

"You won't find it here," said the farmer.

"Do you have any idea where I might look?" asked the boy.

"I'm not sure," said the farmer, rubbing his chin. "But if you do have an idea—any idea—think of it as a seed. Plant the seed and tend it. Soon it will grow and in no time, you will reap the harvest."

Slightly confused, the boy left the farmer.

A while later, he stopped to watch an orchestra playing in the town square. After the performance the young boy spoke to one of the cellos.

"Have you heard anybody sing about the secret of life?" he asked.

"No," said the cello. "But there must be a secret somewhere. Otherwise, how could an old piece of wood like me, with only four strings, make such beautiful music?"

The boy agreed with the cello and
continued his search. He came upon a ladder.

"Have you seen the secret of life?" asked the boy.

"I've been up and I've been down," said the ladder, "but I've never seen the secret of life. I do know the more you climb, the higher you get and the higher you get, the harder you fall. So always make sure of your footing as you climb."

The boy felt frustrated and a little sad. So he went down to the beach, sat on the sand, and stared at the water.

"Don't worry," said the sea. "Think of yourself as an ocean and think of the frustrating things that happen to you as waves. They will pass."

The boy continued his search.
He came across a tortoise.

"I'm looking for the secret of life,"
said the boy.

"Take . . . your . . . time,"

said the tortoise.

"You will . . .

find it."

The boy went home and changed his clothes. He lay on his bed and stared at the ceiling.

"Bad day?" asked the bed.

"Yup," said the boy.

"Take a break," said the bed. "A little rest never harmed anyone."

So the boy took a nap.

When he woke up, he washed his face
and set out to continue his search.

He walked . . . and walked . . . until he came
upon a fence.

"I must find the secret of life," said the boy,
leaning against the fence.

"The secret of life is not one thing," said the fence.

"Take me, for example. Each post means nothing until it is joined to make a long, winding fence. A fence that goes all over the place but stays together."

The boy was so determined to find the secret of life and inherit his grandfather's riches that he left the small town he lived in and searched the earth for the answer.

For years, the boy searched . . .

and searched.

He became a young man . . .

and still he searched.

Eleven years, twelve days, twenty-two minutes, and thirty-six seconds after beginning his search, the young man returned home.

"Grandfather," he said. "I have looked all over the world.

"I went to Europe and Asia, Africa and the Americas.

"I attended the university and earned my master's degree.

"I met many people and learned a great deal, but I simply have not been able to find the secret of life."

"But you did find it," said his grandfather. "Your journey itself **was** the secret of life. And along the way you have learned everything you will need to enjoy a full and rich life."

The young man smiled.

"Now all my riches are your riches," said the old man. And he put his arm around his grandson.

"Where will I find your riches?" said the
young man, not wanting to sound too eager.

"Under the big sky," said his grandfather,
pointing to the horizon. "Under the big sky."